30104

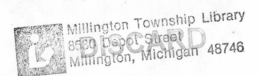
Millington Township Library
8500 Depot Street
Millington, Michigan 48746
DISCARD

E
Enell, Trinka, 1951-
Roll over, Rosie

DEMCO

D1314970

FEB '93

Millington Township Library
8530 Depot Street
Millington, Michigan 48746
DISCARD

ROLL OVER, ROSIE

by Trinka Enell • Illustrated by Dick Gackenbach

CLARION BOOKS • NEW YORK

Clarion Books
a Houghton Mifflin Company imprint
215 Park Avenue South, New York, NY 10003

Text copyright © 1992 by Trinka Enell
Illustrations copyright © 1992 by Dick Gackenbach

All rights reserved.

For information about permission to reproduce selections from
this book, write to Permissions, Houghton Mifflin Company,
2 Park Street, Boston, MA 02108.

Printed in the U.S.A.

Library of Congress Cataloging-in-Publication Data

Enell, Trinka, 1951-
Roll over, Rosie / by Trinka Enell : illustrated by Dick Gackenbach.
    p. cm.
Summary: A girl tries everything to get her dog Rosie to
learn to roll over, from bribery and threats to appealing to
Rosie's pride.
ISBN 0-395-59340-9
[1. Dogs—Fiction.]   I. Gackenbach, Dick, ill.   II. Title.
PZ7.E6967Ro   1992
[E]—dc20   91-34859
                                                        CIP
                                                         AC

WOZ 10 9 8 7 6 5 4 3 2 1

For my mama,
who loves Rosie too.

Wake up, Rosie.
Tomorrow is the dog show.
You have to learn to roll over
if you want to win first prize.

Come on, Rosie.
Don't just sit there
and wag your tail at me.
Roll over!
Please —
I'll give you a yummy dog biscuit.

Millington Township Library
8530 Depot Street
Millington, Michigan 48746

5

There, wasn't that good?

Now, roll over, Rosie.

Rosie!

I didn't say jump on the couch!

I said roll over!

Get off the couch, Rosie!

Rosie — oh, Rosie!

I have something for you in the kitchen!

It tastes delicious, Rosie.

Yum, yum, yum!

7

Come on, Rosie!

You had a whole bowl of dog food.

The least you can do is roll over.

Oh, you want something else?

Some cheese? All right.

But then you have to roll over, Rosie.

There, you had your cheese.

Now . . . One. Two. Three. Roll over!

Don't beg, Rosie, roll over!

9

Rosie! Come back here!

Boy, you are really making me mad!

I mean, you had a biscuit,

and a bowl of yummy dog food,

and a piece of cheese,

and you still won't roll over.

Is that fair?

All right, that's it!
I'm not going to be nice anymore.
Either you roll over right now,
or I'm going to give you a bath.
What do you think of that, Rosie?
You hate baths, Rosie.

Rosie, come out from under that bed!
How can I give you a bath
if you're hiding under the bed?

Millington Township Library
8530 Depot Street
Millington, Michigan 48746

13

Hey, Rosie!

Look what I found.

It's a book about a famous dog named Lady.

Look at all the things she could do!

Wow! She was some dog!

Rosie, don't lie there like a dummy!

Just think, if you won first prize

someone could write a book about you!

Wouldn't that be something?

You'd be famous!

Maybe you'd even be on TV.

Listen, Rosie.

If you don't learn to roll over,

Hector will win first prize.

You don't want Hector to win, do you?

He bites kids.

He chases cats.

He steals your bones.

It would be awful if Hector won.

Look — there he is, next door.

Wow! He's standing on his hind feet!

So come on, Rosie, roll over!

Boy, you sure are a stubborn dog, Rosie.
I know you could do it in a second
if you'd just try.
Here — I'll show you how.

See, that wasn't hard.
Now you try.
Ugh — you are really heavy, Rosie.
There, we did it!
Okay, you do it by yourself now.
Go on, Rosie, roll over!

Rosie, I didn't say shake.

I know you can shake.

Every dog on the block can shake.

That's why you have to learn to roll over.

I just don't understand why you won't try!

Listen, Rosie, first prize

is a fancy red leather collar.

Here's a picture of it in the paper.

It's covered with rubies and diamonds, Rosie!

Boy, you'd look super in that collar.

So roll over, Rosie, please?

25

Well, I think I'll go and see
how Hector is getting along.
See you later, Rosie.

ROWFF!

27

What is it, Rosie?

Rosie!

You rolled over!

Oh, I knew you could do it!

Wait until we show Hector!
My Rosie, queen of the dog show...
Rosie, stop that licking!
Oh, Rosie!

31

Millington Township Library
8530 Depot Street
Millington, Michigan 48746

DISCARD